# Specimen Sight-Reading Tests for Saxophone

## Grades 6–8

**ABRSM**

MIX
Paper from
responsible sources
FSC™ C109619

# GRADE 6

AB 2522

**3** Animato

**4** Steady

**Lento sostenuto**

**5**

**Molto vivo**

**6**

AB 2522

**9** Allegro vigoroso

**10** Allegretto grazioso

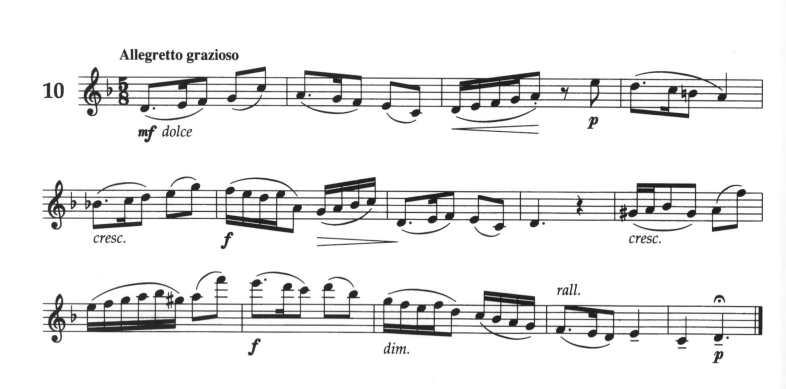

**11**

**12**

**15** Lightly swung

**16** Waltz-time

# GRADE 7

Typeset by Musonix

Printed in England by Caligraving Limited Thetford Norfolk